NOMD

Naturally Occurring Mega Disasters

WILL FIVE TEENS SAVE THE DAY FOR PLANET EARTH?

ARNAB SENGUPTA

Illustrations by

Vaishanavi Vishwanath

DEDICATED

TO

MOTHER EARTH

TABLE OF CONTENTS

When it all began....

I am a crazy sci-fi fan (I guess you can tell!) and I am a stickler for poems and a good plot in a story. That's how NOMD was born! The story shows how 5 teens try to save the world from 'Natural Disasters'. The book also has an element of friendship and also has the element of mystery! The friendship shown in this book is inspired from my life and my friends. The element of mystery, I cannot divulge too much information (otherwise it wouldn't be so mysterious anymore now would it), but I'll tell you something's coming, something big! The element of climate change brings upon another story. Now about me... When I was in one of my former schools, the school was clearing trees to make a big ground. I was really young and I said, *"Don't Do It'* to the woodcutter. I have always been concerned about climate change, pollution, deforestation and the merciless killing of animals. This is my second (so, its chronologically second, but in terms of writing, this is supposed to be my first attempt) attempt on writing a book. I hope you like it! This is Arnab, signing off

Arnab Sengupta

FOREWORD OF HOPE

On the 7th of December 1972 the crew of Apollo 17 took a photo of our planet, it is one of the most reproduced images of all time, it is called The Blue Marble and you have almost certainly seen it. It was the first image that showed our home planet earth as a fully illuminated globe. It helped to change the way humankind saw our home, planet earth. It helped us to understand that we are all part of one ecosystem and that our home is fragile, it helped spawn ideas like Earth Day and helped to build the environmental movement.

Times have changed since 1972, unfortunately not for the better. Our carbon footprint is the highest since records began. We are fast approaching an irreversible climate breakdown so it is how we act now that will define the future of Earth.

I first learned about the impact of The Blue Marble from former Vice President Al Gore when I trained to be a Climate Reality Leader, since then I have spoken to hundreds of businesses, schools, and community groups about the importance of leaving fossil fuels in the ground and moving towards a more sustainable future. We have the solutions now, but we lack the political will to make the systemic change needed for our children and our children's children to look back at us as heroes instead of villains.

I use the words heroes and villains as we will be praised by future generation or vilified by them. I also use the words to draw attention to the importance of storytelling in this battle we find ourselves in.

Living in the UK the climate crisis has a relatively small impact on my life so on my journey I wanted to learn about the stories behind the people most affected by the climate crisis. Quite often some of the poorest people in the world. Telling the story of a farmer in India whose crops have been destroyed by historic flooding and the impact that has on numerous lives often has a greater impact on people than explaining the science. I tell other people's stories to help make a human connection to a crisis that is very difficult to understand, however works of fiction have probably influenced more lives around the globe than anything else, from Shakespeare to 1984 fictional storytelling informs, educates, inspires, entertains and challenges the way we think.

Arnab Sengupta's latest work does exactly this. Anytime you put pen to paper or fingertip to keyboard for a project like Naturally Occurring Mega Disasters you are sharing a part of yourself with the world, so to write a foreword is not just a huge honour it is a huge responsibility.

Naturally Occurring Mega Disasters is a metaphor for what is happening to our planet, it is also a point of view that I think many people of Arnab's age already know ... that we must change now to give them a future. It is a cry for help from our planet but also a desire for equality amongst humankind. We need a new collective consciousness a new vision of hope for the future of our planet, enabled and empowered by exceptional young people like Arnab Sengupta.

James Murphy,

Climate Reality Leader, Social Entrepreneur, Founder of Responsible & Local Business Awards, Co-editor of Future of Earth. ADHD and Neurodiversity advocate, United Kingdom

FOREWORD OF LIGHT

Treat Mother Earth as you would like your Mother to be treated. Protecting our Mother Nature is the responsibility of each and everyone.

These are 2 statements which everyone should internalize – every day since we have only one Planet. Nature gives us everything we need for our existence and living.

I have been honored to know young Mr. Arnab Sengupta for several years now. When he was a teenager, I met him first time here in Bahrain, in a public workshop about IT programming, which he was attending with his parents, I was very impressed by his maturity of the questions he asked and the statements he made during that session.

Expressing my gratitude to his parents about his comments I introduced myself to all of them. After the workshop we had a long chat all together about current and future development of humanity and nature

Born and educated in Germany, an architect and project manager by profession and a nature lover and environmental advocate by passion, I was raised by a single mother as a decent human being, appreciating what we have in life and protecting what gives us everything for living – my mother and our all Mother Nature.

Our family, our friends, our enemies, our societies we live in and our life teaches us many lessons, which we have to learn from on a daily basis and from each other. Age or experience, culture or location, society or community does not matter how and where, but we learn…..We have to learn to grow, as the world is developing faster and faster, and maybe not in the best direction; but the direction is in our hand to make the world and to make our Mother Earth a better place for the future generations to come.

Since ever our first meeting I am following the personal development of Arnab by staying in touch with his father, who helped me as well a lot for some publications. Keeping connection with outstanding personalities and exchange views and experience will help everyone to grow; hence I am much honored to write this foreword for his book NOMD "Naturally Occurring Mega Disaster" which shows the smartness of the outstanding young personality - Arnab Sengupta.

The book deals with the fiction of waves of natural disasters occurring as a threat to humanity, which are created by an evil organization. Unfortunately, that scenario became already real nowadays and these disasters are happening in reality due to the climate change. The five teenagers who are trying to save the world reflecting the part of our current society who really care about the planet and are passionate about preserving Mother nature, like Arnab. Whereas the evil organization, which are creating these disasters are the part of humanity caring only about themselves, believing in wrong values and destroying the lifeline and base of living of human being for their EGO.

The teenagers are like some of the typical young and curious humane group of friends, innocent and wondering what the future will provide them. Their curiosity and excitement about the unknown lets them start investigating on what is happening with the world due to the "Naturally Occurring Mega Disasters", which are not natural, but caused by humans, evil humans. So, what else energetic and passionate young people will do than trying to save the world?

Climate change is the current reality and not fiction anymore. We are all in this together and everyone has got the responsibility to do her or his share. Not as a onetime action, it must be happening on a daily basis, and with an effort that really helps to change society, their habits, the mindset and behavior of each and every one, on a daily basis for the future of humanity.

Let us all be the like the five teenagers against this evil organization to combat climate change and destruction of Mother Earth.

Let us all help the society to change from those evil habits of EGO, carelessness and convenience to become caring, decent human beings preserving Mother Nature and our all-planet Earth to ensure a better future for the generations to come.

This book will support the idea of changing mindsets of readers and start evaluating your own daily habits, making it less harmful for the environment, and investigating on what big parts of society and many companies, those "evil organizations" are actually doing to our all-Mother Nature for the sake of profit, EGO and convenience.

Arnab Sengupta is like one of the 5 teenagers with passion and an investigative mindset to question and research on what and why disasters are happening, so let us all be like them. Not just accepting what happening but finding out the reason and developing a solution for a change.

Be the change you want to see in the world. Be investigative, be curios, be decent, be protective, be inspirational, be like those teenagers, be like Arnab Sengupta and influence society and humanity for a better future of the generations to come.

Thank you again Arnab Sengupta to give me the honor writing this foreword and I hope, no I am sure, with every book, you will change the mindset of your readers and the society.

Stay safe and an inspiring role model for your generation and the generations to come.

Kai Miethig

German architect, environmental advocate and efficiency consultant

Thanks.

It is a powerful word, that can change the hearts of the most villainous heart, and touch the souls of all. It is a weapon of kindness, that could turn mean people into people who actually mean something to others. So, I would like to say this word to a few people, who made this book possible.

Thanks, Mom and Dad, for a multitude of reasons. The most important reason is a cliched one, but nonetheless a foundation for this and hopefully upcoming work, and that is – Support. You supported me through every single step. If I was the pen, you were the ink! Thank you for your love and support. Thanks for being my ma and baba.

Thanks to James Murphy, for being one of the first people to give me a platform to speak, to express my ideas. Also, thanks for writing the Foreword of Hope. Thank you for always supporting me and being there in my life

Thanks to Kai Miethig, for being so kind so as to talk with me during that Google I.O. meet. Since then, we have talked about the sustainable ways we can save the world. Thanks for believing in me, for writing the Foreword of Light and for being there in this journey, with me

Thanks to the illustrator of this book, Vaishnavi Vishwanathan. Her art is a perfect supplement to the story, depicting the story in detail. Thanks as well to Radha for contributing her beautiful sketch for my book.

Thank you to my family, for always giving me constructive feedback, that helped me improve the book. you, for the love and the kind words!

Lastly, thanks to everyone who has been, is, and will be, in my life, since I have always learnt something new from everyone (and I am trying to learn more from the people I have interacted with.) Thanks to all of you!

Arnab Sengupta
3rd Nov. 2021/Bahrain

WHEN WORLDS COLLIDE

A LIGHT SHINES SO BRIGHT

IT IS AN AMAZING SIGHT

WHEN THE LIGHT TAKES A BITE

OUT OF THE GLOOMY PLIGHT

OF PEOPLE SO NICE

WHY DO THEY HAVE TO PAY THE PRICE?

BUT BRIGHTNESS THE PROTECTOR

SAVES THIS SECTOR

OF GLOOMINESS WHICH FILLS EVERY HECTARE

BUT THAT'S NOT THE STORY

WHICH HAS A LOT OF GLORY

A STORY OF TWO WORLDS

WHICH I HAVE OBSERVED

AND KEPT IT PRESERVED

THIS IS THE STORY

WHICH IS NOT SO IMAGINARY

INTRODUCTION TO THE CHARACTERS
Hamid Shah

Hamid Shah, a 13-year-old boy from <u>THE PINK CITY,</u> is a very talented Sufi singer. He is the youngest Sufi singer in the world. He had first lived in a small village in Jaisalmer. His parents were very poor, and they lived in a small mud dome. His father was a small-time labourer and his mother, a maid in the big city houses. Hamid always wanted to be a singer, but his parents did not have any money to send him to a music class or enrol him in a good school. Then how did he become so famous? He sang for his village every weekend during village *chaupati* gatherings. Some days later, a Sufi troupe was passing by that village. Coincidentally, Hamid was performing at the same time. The troupe heard his voice and asked if he wanted to join them on their journey to Indian Idol and he said yes! His parents though did not agree so easily, as they were worried about his safety. The Sufi artists assured that they would take full care of him. After a lot of convincing, his parents said yes! His journey to the top three was a long one, but the result was sweet! He had won the prize and also had taken the offer of working with the famous music director duo, Vishal-Shamar. That's how he became a hotshot!!

Sophia Little

Sophia Little is a very intelligent 10-year-old kid from Alaska who became the youngest meteorologist in the world! Her story of success is something like Hamid Shah's. Only here the troupe of artistes was replaced by a group of scientists who were studying the landform and other geographical and meteorological elements of Alaska. Sophia was just a kid back then, when this happened. She was about 10 years old, maybe but she could predict the next day's weather without any complex equations of any kind. She knew how the clouds actually worked like the back of her hand. She was interviewed by the local newspaper and also by the local television channel. Word about the unique ability of Sophia started spreading far and wide. When a group of scientists passed through the small-town Sophia lived in, they searched for her and came to meet her. The meteorologists were very curious as of how she was able to do so. When they asked her, she said that she used to observe the clouds when it poured or snowed and when it was pleasant, and then she started to understand how the weather changes. They took her under their wing and that's how, at 13 years of age, she can predict the weather a month in advance! She even made the career of her father Buck Little, earlier a small time engineer and currently the CEO of BuckTech.

The Friends

Dr Akshay Gupta, Quantum Astrophysicist – This 11-year-old boy is the quantum astrophysicist at NERN and the chief astrophysicist in Team X (A group strictly created to end the Naturally Occurring Mega Disasters (NOMD - more about this in the later chapters). The 'boy wonder' shot to fame after he had written a research paper with the late Stephen Hawqueen! The theoretical physicist noticed this tiny gleaming star when he visited the International Centre for Biology and Quantum

Physics, where the kid used to attend lectures and do experiments. The scientist noticed him there when he was giving a lecture to the students. He then invited the little kid to NERN to write a research paper with him and he was obviously honoured to do that! He then became more known in the world of science, as the research paper was read by hundreds of quantum physicists around the world. He had written the research paper on the space time continuum and the effects of bending it! He is home-schooled on quantum physics and only attends lectures outside. He is very fond of dogs and dislikes cats (no offense!) He is actually the 'boy wonder' that all the newspapers talk about. A great mathematician and quantum physicist, he is one of the smartest kids in the world, with an IQ of 500. He was also given an honorary doctorate by MiiT.

-Dr Keerth D.S, Mechanical Physicist and Mechanical Quantumizing Physicist — A mechanical engineer by profession, this 13-year-old genius are a fantastic physicist, and this is how he shot to fame: Mohit and Keerth had been to several science competitions and won them all! One such competition changed Keerth's life forever! The Indian Institute Of Mechanical and Climate Technology's Biannual Science Competition is one of the most prestigious competitions. They participated with Keerth as their leader. They called their Project '768'. It was basically a hard disk containing 768 gegobytes (10 to the power of 30 bytes) of storage space as the pre-loaded storage space. That's bigger than the storage space of all of the storing disks of the world multiplied by infinity! All of this fit into a small pen-drive! Yes! One pen-drive like device! They called it the

AKM 768. They obviously won the prize, but Keerth was noted for his work on nanotizing a device capable to hold so much data. He was then given an honorary degree and doctorate from MiiT! Then he went to join NERN, which he was successful in. He is now a mechanical quantumizing physicist.

Dr. Mohit Kumar – A people's man, he is the one who makes everyone laugh. Due to this, no one ever took him seriously. But, little did they know, that this boy was an amazing guy! In the same competition that made Keerth a hotshot, this future star was found. He was the coder behind the MegaBank (Also known as the AKM 768, the K and the M standing for Keerth and Mohit, respectively and the A for Hmm, I don't know?)! The judges asked the question that who had coded the storage system into the MegaBank and we all pointed towards Mohit. They asked him how he did it and he answered, "I had closely investigated different hard disks and storage systems and then understood that I needed a series of codes, pre-written by me. The code can be tweaked to increase or decrease the storage! The gegabytes is just the pre-loaded storage as the storage can be increased or decreased indefinitely!" The judges were impressed and he was also given and honorary doctorate by MiiT and, was invited to program the QuantumSuper, the fastest computer in the world's storage system! Now, he still goes to school as he thinks proper schooling helps in many things. He now is no longer taunted by his classmates. Instead, they now see him as an inspiration!

The Villain and His Syndicate Army

ICS – The International Criminal Syndicate is a criminal organization comprising of the greatest supervillains of the world. This syndicate, created in 1340 during the Renaissance period, included the criminals BioHazard and BrainStorm. The ICS has caused all of the crimes in the world since it's creation. The founder of the syndicate, MegaGrandMaster Mal Malevolent had a traumatic backstory, like all criminals do. When he was a child, he became an orphan. He was raised by criminals who led to the creation of the ICS! One of the most popular criminals was Mark Fuller, or as they called him, BioHazard.

BioHazard-An alias of the notorious scientist Mark Fuller, the name would terrify all of the smaller criminals in the ICS. He was a board member of the ICS. He headed their biggest mission ever, the 'NOMD'. He was a good person, before the EcoTop (You will read about this afterwards), which was a billion-dollar idea. The greed made him into a criminal and he then joined the ICS, where he was part of many missions, due to his incredible knowledge of Bioweapons, hence he adopted the alias BioHazard

The Complimentary Narrator – Mariachi Band

WE ARE THE MARIACHI BAND

WE GIVE THE AUTHOR A HAND

TO MAKE THIS STORY BEAUTIFUL

AND ALSO, VERY, VERY COOL

Hmm, what are you guys doing here

WE HEARD OF THIS STORY

YOU KNOW, THE ONE NOT SO IMAGINARY

AND WE WERE CURIOUS, SO WE CAME TO SEE

WHO WAS THIS PERSON, AND HOW COULD WE ACCOMPANY?

So, to be honest. The role of narrator is kinda fulfilled by me. Don't you agree, Readers?

THE READER- True, but I mean, you could get them to accompany you. And kinda enhance the story with their small songs. You know, just like soap opera's always put some kind of music in the background to enhance the drama.

True. That's very much true. Thanks for the suggestion, Reader. I will accept it!

THE READER- No worries. Looking forward to the story of this universe

Me too. Anyways, Mariachi Band, let's begin.

NOW WE SHALL BEGIN

THE JOURNEY THAT NEEDED TO START

LET'S STOP TALKING LIKE ROBOTS OF TIN

AND BEGIN THIS EMOTIONAL ROLLERCOASTERS, WITH FLAVOURS SALTY, SWEET AND TART.

Can you guys please tone it down? It would be nice. In text, that's done by switching to Sentence Case

Okay.

Now let's not waste the day

Let's begin with 'Once Upon a Time'

And let the knowledge shine

Chapter 1

Where and When It All Began

Hamid was walking down the road with 'Apna Time Apnayega' blasting in his headphones. He was heading to his friend, Shaan's house {Not the singer!!}. He and Shaan met on the sets of Indian Idol. They were very good friends from then. Shaan lived just a few blocks away from Hamid. He was going there for an Xbox One Showdown!! When they turned on the television, accidentally it switched to the news channel.

Shaan was desperately trying to change the channel when they saw the news, showing that an Armageddon was coming - A combination of all Disasters were going to come in a year and a quarter of the world's population would be affected by that. The news reporter also said that a tidal wave was coming, which would flood the entire world! The chief scientist of the group 'Adults Team' announced that they are

They had nicknamed it the NOMD or the Naturally Occurring Mega Disasters. They also announced that they had checked the clouds and said that it showed some unknown readings but, they did not care for it as they thought it was just a disturbance. Shaan then switched to the Xbox One port and they started playing. Shaan ignored the news and also told Hamid to do so as well. He said that these meteorologists always made bad predictions and this was one of them. He told Hamid to not fall for this.

collaborating with BuckTech (You'll know about it in the later chapters) to try to avert the Disasters to affect the world.

They ignored the news

They had different views

After all, they had to play Xbox One

To worry about this, they had days a ton

Sophia on the other hand, was very worried. She was checking where the Naturally Occurring Mega Disasters would occur. She then saw that it would majorly affect the whole of Alaska, some parts of Europe and some parts of Asia but she couldn't pinpoint the exact locations where it would actually affect. She also found out that it was not a year away; it was only a week away!! How to stop this from happening was the question. She had then tried to work out a solution for the whole day, as she could not get any sleep. At last, she found a solution. To expel this force, they would need a barrier that would not only neutralise the NOMD; it would also protect the places which would be affected largely in a week's time. She knew how to build this machine but she needed some help. She did tell her parents and the other scientists, who worked in BuckTech but unfortunately, they did not believe her. But her predictions about the NOMD were right, but the other scientists (burning with jealousy, I must say), said it was just a fluke. Sophia predicted that the NOMD was approaching fast, really fast. She requested her parents, Mr Buck Little and Mrs. Susanne Little, to understand her and help her save the world, but the problem was that no one could fathom the idea of a child to save the world. So they wouldn't believe her, but she

always was right, and the scientists would never listen to her. But she would try and try. A fighting spirit was Sophia

The adults did not think of the idea seriously and did not take Sophia seriously either and said yes at that time but she had a feeling that this was all fake. Just to check, she eavesdropped on the conversation of the adults, which went something like this. *"Sophia might have become a famous meteorologist but she's still a kid, huh"* Zamno Zapper, the famous electrical engineer said to which Zander Axtell, the famous astronomer, said, *"Yes, she so kiddish, She still dreams big"*. This was enough to prove to her that the adults wouldn't believe her yet again. She murmured to herself, "The adults will never listen to me. But maybe, kids might! And there are some people in the world, who can help me. The true heroes of the world are children after all" And she was adamant, and was sure that she wanted kid heroes in the team, kids who had done notable things in science or had the capability to understand science, kids who had the capability to fund this project and some amazing leaders.

The help she received

Was from a person you couldn't imagine

When you will hear his name, you'll be shocked to disbelief

It might feel like magic!!

Chapter 2

THE DREAM TEAM!

Hamid was not only an expert Sufi singer; He was also an expert engineer. In Jaisalmer, he worked in a mechanic shop, and he also got the chance to build car parts and bikes too!! After winning the Indian Idol contest he was admitted in a good school in Jaipur. The talents he possessed were innumerable. His talent of engineering came to light in his current school when he participated in a science competition and his team won the first prize!! Since then, Hamid started taking part in many competitions and also started going to tech meetups and because of that, he had learnt a lot about technology. Then, he went for a competition which happened in the city of FloRidea. It was called 'Young Innovation' and was held by Googol to find kids who had a great potential and could do a lot in the technology field. The first prize for the competition was that the winning team would be inducted into Googol as paid interns; the project would be launched by Googol and a cash prize of 40000000 dollars! Hamid and team won the contest with their 'Bio-Bot'! Now, Hamid is an intern with Googol along with his team!

After returning from Shaan's house, he started watching the news and saw Sophia give a speech to the Junior Team or Team X, as they called it, about her plan (Backstory, after the party night, the next day she prepared a speech which she was adamant that she would present it in the press conference that would happen at London. Her parents did not want her to

give the speech and make a joke out of them. They refused many times until Sophia persuaded them to listen to her speech. After they heard her speech, they felt inspired. This speech impressed her parents quite a bit and they asked her a few questions, just like the press would on that day. After she successfully answered each and every one of them, her dad said, "I knew that those guys did not know you. I always deep down knew you would one day be a leader. But that fact that you are already one, makes me proud. I, and BuckTech, and your dear Mom, will support you in every way. Now let's go to London!"

London was an interesting city. Cloudy, but beautiful, nonetheless. Sophia, though felt concerned when looking at those clouds. Her dad asked her carefully, "What's the matter, Sophia?" Sophia replied, "I feel concerned about everything. I'm trying to keep my wits, but I feel terrified." Her dad said, "Look, it is natural to feel afraid. What you can do with this fear, is that be inspired by it, work to beat the fear. Do so, and things will soon change." Sophia felt a sense of responsibility and started her action plan.

 She first called Team X's chosen members and asked them if they were coming to the press conference and all of these contacts said yes. It wasn't an easy task convincing the scientists, but they were convinced, but wanted to shift the conference to NERN. Sophia happily agreed but decided to stay for a day and do a press release. The press release was given throughout the world, giving information about the NOMD, and how they were looking for volunteers to fight it. Hamid saw this press release on the newspaper. Hamid knew what machine to make but he did not know how to contact the team. He then searched on the internet for the website and then he found it. The URL of the website was: -

www.nomd.in

He then registered and an interview followed. This is how Sophia and Hamid finally talked to each other. Sophia asked a few questions. The conversation followed like this: -

Sophia – *Hello, Mr. Hamid Shah.*

Hamid – *Hello Ms Sophia.*

Sophia – *How many years old are you?*

Hamid – *I'm 13.*

Sophia – *Where do you live?*

Hamid – *The pink city, Jaipur! It's in Rajasthan, which is a state in India.*

Sophia – *Do you have any scientific background?*

Hamid – *I have won many awards in science competitions and am also currently the youngest intern in Googol.*

Sophia – *Impressive! What do you intern for in Googol?*

Hamid – *I specialise in the coding of the Googol's AI for the assistant.*

Sophia – *Nice! How much is your salary?*

Hamid – *That's kind of personal, don't you think? And how does joining the team related to my salary?*

Sophia – *True. I was asking this question just so I can know if you can fund this project or not.*

Hamid - *I will fund the project!*

Sophia – *Thanks! The last question is – Why do you want to join this project?*

Hamid – *I guess because I'm scared that the whole of Rajasthan will be destroyed by the NOMD and as that is where most of my family lives in, I fear that I will lose them!*

Sophia – *I understand. So, this is it! We'll call you later! Bye!*

Hamid – *Bye!*

Sophia was now almost done with her Phase 1. The press conference would happen in the headquarters of NERN, in Geneva, Switzerland, The invitees were -Her father, Mr Buck Little, who was a major investor in the project and convinced all of the other invitees that the kids had capabilities; her mother, Mrs Susanne Little, who was the CEO of BuckTech, which made much technological advancement in the world. She had come to support Sophia, the teams of Googol, Microsoft and Apple and obviously, the heads of all the countries. Oh, I forgot to mention The UN. All of them were called by special request of Sophia, conveyed by her parents. And obviously, THE TEAM. Now what Sophia needed was a group of kid scientists and a kid chief engineer, who would supervise the project. Interview after interview followed, many people were inducted to the team and some were rejected. After this, ten thousand scientists were inducted into the group and Sophia thought that would be enough. Five hundred of them were the earlier members of Team X, who volunteered in taking interviews. Most of them were the kids inducted into the team after the interviews. She could have taken all of the members from BuckTech but, she wanted to get the best talent and so, she interviewed kids who had achieved a lot in scientific fields, and they wanted some candidates to be from financially strong backgrounds, so that they could fun the projects. They made a website and that's where the interviews were held. The first APEX paragons were chosen. And they were.

- *Keerth D.S – Chief Physics Officer*
- *Mohit Kumar – Chief People's Officer & Chief Programmer*
- *Akshay Gupta – Chief Astrophysics Officer*
- *Hamid Shah- Chief Engineer and Financer*
- *Sophia Little- Chief Climate Officer*

Now all they needed was a chief engineer and some scientists. The material scientists were arranged but the chief engineer was remaining. Out of 10 candidates, one was chosen [Obviously!]. Guess who that was – Hamid!! He was given the chance to come to NERN as he was the best candidate, according to Sophia. He was very excited to finally go to Switzerland, even though it was for official purposes! His parents were hesitant to let him go to NERN, but he persuaded them by explaining that it was his duty to save the world.

THE TEAM WAS COMING TOGETHER

IT WAS ONCE IN FOREVER

BY CHANCE, THEY MEET

READER, RELAX AND HAVE A SEAT

Chapter 3

The Silence Before the Storm

You might have been thinking that it's too easy, too easy for the NOMD; But it wasn't, trust me. What followed will prove my point – The Armedegeddon had begun one day early [That is why never trust meteorologists' prediction]. Also known as the NOMD, phase one was THE STORM which hit the tropical and subtropical regions of Asia, mainly India. The affected places were: -

- Bengaluru
- Colombo
- Jaipur
- Kuala Lumpur
- Mumbai

- Hanoi
- Delhi
- Manila
- Kolkata

(While it was kind of unlikely that heavy rain occurred in a desert, it was just, still natural, at least according to "God's Plan", I guess)

[P.S -The concentration of polluting gases in Delhi had changed the rain into really strong Acid Rain which started burning houses and some people died due to this phenomenon, but we will come to this point later]

The sudden outpour of heavy rain meant that the whole of Rajasthan was flooded and most of Rajasthan's population was either washed away by the flood or trapped in their houses. All the flights were cancelled. Luckily, Hamid's extended family had already left Rajasthan, after Hamid's parents told them about the NOMD. Hamid too had boarded a flight but this one was going to Geneva, Switzerland.

NERN was located just 15 miles away from the hotel in which the accommodations were set. Hamid, Shaan and their parents {Shaan and his family were going to Switzerland and after that, to France, as that felt as the safest place for the moment} had a layover in London when the real storm broke; A call came and the relative on the other line had said that

Aamir, Hamid's cousin, and his family had perished in the Delhi storm. Hamid and his family felt numb and then broke into tears as they were really close to each other. Hamid and Aamir were always onto some kind of a prank whenever they met. He had not only lost his brother; he had lost his partner in crime. He was really sad, but he had to move on, the flight was in 10 minutes. His parents told his son to return to Delhi, but he persuaded them to come with him as these rituals couldn't bring Aamir and his family back. They agreed, with hesitance.

Sophia had also lost someone close to her, her sister, who always gave her good advice and helped whenever she had a dilemma. She went to Delhi to complete her higher studies but unfortunately, this happened, and Sophia's sister succumbed to the acid rain burns. Sophia mourned for a long time in her cabin with her family providing consolation to the little girl. Then, Sophia burst on her parents, saying," Why didn't you listen to me sooner! Why did you trust some strangers over

your own blood!? You should have listened to me sooner. If you did, Sis would be alive today!" She cried, and her parents consoled her. Her dad said, "Don't worry, now that we do listen to you, we wont let others die. We will do this for her. We will save the world for her." Sophia felt a bit better, and felt even more determined to fight this war against NOMD.

Both of them had a score to settle

The steam got out of the kettle

The rage was rising little by little

After all, they had a score to settle

Sketch by **Radha Mahor**, Pathshala Pathbhavan Srotoshwini Trust (NGO), Vadodara, India.

Chapter 4

The Meeting

Hamid had just reached Geneva and was all ready to go to NERN. He was about to attend the introduction event where the team members would be familiarising with each other (for

attendees' list, go to Chapter 2). The Adults team were suspended from working and their project was scraped. The teams of NAGA and NERN would work with Team X in their operation and the invitees to the conference would also fund and also help in the operation. Hamid and his family, along with Shaan had reached the hotel, which was a 5-star hotel and immediately when they entered, they found a chocolate parlour right there. Hamid bought a pack of them, ate them and kept a few for later. When he looked at the 5-star presidential Swiss suites, he was in love with it. It had a Jacuzzi, a bathtub, a hot tub, a mini gym, a computer and gaming room, a living room decorated with sofas and gold and diamond encrusted framed TVs, two bedrooms with TVs made with pure silver and one soft, memory foam bed and Wi-Fi with smart home system. It also had the smart home speakers to control them all! He felt really pampered. But this wasn't the time to be pampered, he said to himself. It was the time to fight against this evil NOMD which had taken his cousin's life. He was filled with rage again!! He then left for the event to discuss the plans and all other scientific things.

Sophia had taken accommodations in the same hotel and was experiencing the same as Hamid. Though both of their rooms were right next to each other, they did not meet at that time in that hotel. Sophia had left earlier than Hamid and had already reached NERN. She was pacing back and forth nervously in the hall.

Then the guests came. The introductory speech was given by Sophia. She said *"Good Morning, Honourable Guests and Team X. Today, we have a big problem to face, a problem that could destroy the world! If we don't do something quickly, innocent lives could be lost. Due to the increased pollution and heavy rains in Delhi, my sister was killed by this horrid disaster. This is what keeps me up at night and breaks me. But it also gives me the determination to fight this horrid disaster, to save the innocent from being killed! That is why I have called all of you here to solve this problem as one, as a team!! As TEAM X!!"* Everyone clapped.

The next speech was by Hamid, the chief engineer. Everyone except Sophia had thought that this kid was some 'village boy' who couldn't speak fluent English, but it was quite the opposite as he had learnt fluent English after he started going to

school. His accent was great, His vocabulary and diction was like an Englishman!! His speech was something like this, *"Greetings my friends. I see that we have such honourable guests in front of us. Don't worry my friends as today I'll be sharing my action plan for how to counter the NOMD. First, we need to deploy mini satellites which can help us monitor the condition of the NOMD. Second, we need to get all the radio waves at one place, the metal matrix covered glass dome, which we also need to deploy. Third, we need to evacuate the people to another place if something goes wrong. I can make all of this happen in a day if all of you support me. Thanks for this opportunity."* Again, everybody in the room had clapped. Then, it was time for the press conference, where the plans were discussed thoroughly and everyone gave their own views, which were all acknowledged. The adults then understood their mistake and started working with the kids. The press was there too, giving the action plan to the people, and questioning the conference, to help improve them and their decisions. It felt like Armageddon was going to lose its arm and the humans would triumph once again.

The plans were made

A lot of things were said

Everybody had come here to save the world

Here at the headquarters of NERN

Chapter 5

They Finally Meet!!

Hamid was back in his hotel room. He lay there on the soft, soft bed and Shaan on the sofa and they just turned on the TV. After some time, he started to wonder where had his and Shaan's parents gone. He had stepped outside of the room to look for them. Sophia, in the next room, was just researching and making a lot of calls to the investors and the scientists too so that she could start executing the plan right away. After all of the researching and calling she made, she stepped

out of the room to clear her head and think clearly. Just as she stepped out of her room, she was knocked over by an unknown person. When she woke up, she saw Hamid standing next to her. Hamid was repeatedly sitting and standing up with his hands on his ears, a universal gesture for apologies, for what he did but Sophia still felt a concussion-like blur and ringing. When she could make out things, she forgave Hamid and asked him why he was running in the corridor. He replied, "I was tired of watching the telly so I decided to jog a bit in the corridors". Sophia laughed and told him, "Don't jog in the corridors, silly! Do it in the jogging track"? Hamid then started the conversation about where he was from and his

hobbies and stuff. He also asked Sophia to do the same and she also told. After that, they shared the sad events. It went something like this: -

Hamid- *What gave you the zest to fight the NOMD?*

Sophia – *At first, the end of the world, obviously and then, the passing of my sister.*

Hamid – *I'm so sorry to hear that…*

Sophia - *It's okay. What about you?*

Hamid – *The thought of my relatives who could get affected by this, which later became into a fear after I lost my cousin. I had actually said this before in the interview if you remembered. And my passion of Sufi is still there! I rehearse every morning with a different practice regime every day.*

Sophia – *I'm sorry for your loss.* And I totally understand

Hamid – *it's okay, thanks. And I know you do. We are fellow victims. We will fight this. Like I do with my Sufi, and well, this project.*

Sophia – *About your practice of Sufi, it's amazing! I heard your music in a video. It was really amazing! Keep it up!*

Hamid – *Thanks, I will.*

Sophia – *What about Googol, I heard you were a paid intern.*

Hamid – *Yes, it happened a year ago.*

Sophia – *Nice! Work Hard. Best of Luck!*

Hamid- *I will!*

Sophia – *So, are we friends now?*

Hamid – *Analysing the ongoing conversation, I'd say yes!*

Sophia-Well, then let's shake hands

(They shake hands)

Hamid- Its nice to have a friend like you.

Sophia-(blushing slightly)- Thanks. Same here

Hamid- Oh, before I forget I transferred the funds to the account.

Sophia – *Thanks! See you tomorrow at NERN but if you want to jog, there's a jogging track.*

Hamid – [Giggling] *Thanks! Bye!*

Sophia – [smiling and giggling] *Bye!!*

Then, Hamid went to his room, satisfied and happy as he had gotten a new friend. But was sad that Shaan was going to go after dinner to France! Shaan went away and so, he weighed the options. He hadn't lost or gained anything, he just was as he was, friendship wise.

THE DESTINED – TO- BE- FRIENDS FINALLY MEET

GOD'S PLAN WORKED A TREAT

IT'S A BIG FEAT

MAKING THE DESTINED MEET

Chapter 6

The Drought

The next day, the next phase had started – THE DROUGHT, which had affected the places the storm had come. It also affected Switzerland and some parts of the Scandavian

countries too. The granaries and farms of these areas were immensely affected. The supply of food supplies was cut down due to this Disasters, which would mean that many people would starve to death!! Luckily, the hotel where Team X was staying had enough supplies to survive for a week. But what about the unlucky ones? For that cause, an Immediate Response Unit was set, and supplies were ordered from

Canada and New Zealand as both of these countries had the ability to mass produce the food supplies. These food supplies were supplied to the affected areas within a day as all of the countries which were expected to be affected by the NOMD, were asked to subscribe to all activities of Team X during the NOMD. Even during the floods caused in Phase 1, The International Response Unit (IRU) was there, as the unofficial agreement had taken place a day or two before NOMD had even begun!!

Hamid woke up the next morning, got dressed, and then reported to NERN HQ, He saw Sophia talking to Akshay {check Chapter 2} about

Mission Small Step, Big Step, which was basically a way to monitor the NOMD, using small satellites, which were made using biodegradable materials. He overheard their conversation which went something like this: -

Akshay-*Ma'am We are launching the satellites today and also launching the applications in the NOMD – affected countries*

Sophia – *Good Job, Akshay!!*

Akshay – *Thanks, ma'am!!*

Sophia – *Where is your team?*

Akshay – *Actually, Hamid sir hasn't briefed us yet and also hasn't spoken to us about when the launch should happen and so that's why I haven't called my team yet.*

Sophia – *You do know that you could have contacted Hamid sir, right?*

Akshay – *I did call him, ma'am but he did not answer.*

Sophia – *Oh! In that case, I'll contact him. If he doesn't pick up, I will be taking temporary command of Mission Small Step, Big Step, is that clear?*

Akshay – *Yes ma'am!!*

Sophia – *You are free to go.*

Akshay – *Thanks ma'am.*

Just then, Sophia spotted Hamid and then another conversation erupted, which went something like this -

Sophia – {Angrily} *Where were you for so long? You're late!! Your team member – Akshay, has called you so many times, but you didn't answer any of the calls that he made. Why? You know how much this project is vital for the success of averting any damage that could be caused by the NOMD, and you were informed about the timings. Then why did you come late?*

Hamid – Sorry, ma'am. Actually, there was a huge delay with the driver as he came approximately… 30 minutes late and after all that, he took the route which takes longest time to reach NERN, which is approximately 1 hour. And about my phone, it ran out of charge as yesterday I had drained all of the charge by playing- I mean, researching and calling others for research, you know. And, to take a break I was calling and chatting with my friends who live near my vicinity, and play games. Ok fine, I mostly played Road Tire 5. I did some research too.

Sophia – Ok, be a bit responsible *and from next time, please charge your phone and ask your driver to come early, okay? And stop calling me ma'am – you're of my age.*

Hamid – *Okay, but as you are much senior in position, it's wrong to call you just Sophia.*

Sophia – *I admire your respect towards me and fellow co-workers but, please don't call me Maam. To actually give me respect, come on time and play a bit less games, is that clear!*

Hamid – Yes, *Sophia.*

Sophia – *Now, go! You should brief your teammates*

Hamid – *Yes! Ok bye, Sophia!*

Sophia – *Bye, Hamid!*

Hamid then started briefing his team -*"Team, Today is a very big day for Operation 'Paragon X' as we are launching the network of small monitoring satellites and the interactive interfaces or apps, as the common man calls it- are going to be launched today so, I want all of you to do your job properly. The whole world depends on it, okay team?*

They all replied with a resounding 'yes!' .Akshay, start the countdown in an hour. *Keerth, do last minute 500 steps check, quickly! Mohit, check if the codes are written properly and debug if any bugs are found and rest of you, help the officers* to complete their respective duties, is that clear?" They all reply, "yes, sir!" "Now, man your stations, quickly!!

The launch was successful and the monitoring systems, with the apps were up in about 3 hours after the launch.

THE THINGS WERE COMING

TOGETHER

MANY RESOURCES HAD ALREADY BEEN GATHERED

THE SATELLITES WERE NOW SCATTERED

BUT WHAT CAME NEXT MADE THE GOOD THING A HAZARD

Chapter 7

Troubleshooting

The next day, Keerth was monitoring the SNOMDMS when the whole system went offline! He then discussed this with Hamid and Mohit

Keerth – *The SNOMDMS has gone blind!*

Hamid – *Did you do the 500-step check?*

Keerth – *Yes, sir! I did the 500-step check 500 times!*

Mohit – *And I also checked the codes, and they were pretty normal.*

Hamid – *Ok. That means it's not the fault of you two. Is hacking into the system possible?*

Mohit – *Very difficult, but possible! The firewall encryption is really thick so, I don't think that breaking in the system would be easy. Only a professional hacker can decrypt the system very easily as there is a hack tool called as Decrypt$nake, which can decrypt upto 10^{13} firewalls in 1 millisecond!*

Hamid – *Did you check for any bugs after this happened?*

Keerth – *No, doing it now!*

(Keerth searched and searched and looked shocked)

Hamid- What did you find, Keerth?

Keerth- I checked for bugs and what I found was really shocking! I found the Decrypt$nake tool in the system just before it shut down completely!

Hamid — *How did you do it without electricity?*

Keerth — *Well, I had installed a 10^{12} Gegowatts emitting solar generator functioning at full capacity!*

Hamid — *Why didn't you say so?*

Keerth — *You never asked!*

Hamid — *Mechanic, connect the building with the solar generator!*

[Mechanic joined the conversation]

Mechanic — *Yes sir!*

[Mechanic left the conversation]

Hamid — *Let's inform Sophia about this problem.*

What actually happened now was that somebody had installed a virus to the monitoring system which destroyed all the code and made the satellites nothing but a big hunk of useless metal. That wasn't the only effect — It was found that all of the electricity of the world had been utilised by the satellites mysteriously. How could this happen? The electricity used by these satellites was quite less!! There is sabotage!! The person who did this wanted to not only blackout the whole world, but also wanted the NOMD to succeed! Who did this?

They were eager to find answers but right now they had no time to worry about the project as the NOMD's third wave was approaching and the SNOMDMS was down! Team X's engineering team, led by Hamid, focused on reviving the SNOMDMS while the humanitarian and scientific research

team led by Sophia, focused on the supplying of medicines and supplies {Yes, medicines were needed as next came Phase Three – The Infection]

The SNOMDMS was back online within an hour due to the efficiency of the Engineering Team and the supplies were supplied within a day due to efficiency of the Humanitarian Team. Both teams had done their troubleshooting and were now relaxed, only for a moment as the saboteur was still out there {Saboteur – a person who sabotages things]. The investigation was taken up by Interpol who tried to find out who the heck was it!

About two years ago, when the NOMD was a distant fear, Sophia was working on a project called the EcoTop with her friend and scientist, Mark Fuller, who was the biochemist at NERN. Mark was 18! He loved to observe how viruses work and he loved to see the destruction they made. Kind of weird for a scientist who is working for a good cause, isn't it? Anyways, Mark and Sophia had completed the project and Sophia wanted to sell the idea to Googol, but Mark here had some other plans!

Sophia and Mark were just sitting there, in the lobby, sipping on their favourite, Hot Cocoa. After that, Sophia stared to feel a pain in her chest. Slowly, she started to cough and with each cough, came a bit of blood and after a few moments, she went unconscious! Mark had mixed a virus, .exe, which could kill a person, by multi-organ failure, if not treated, in 2 hours! And it would have been the case if the head scientist at NERN, Mr Zurek Vladavitch, was not there He had identified the .exe virus and got Sophia treated immediately. This was just a diversion as Mark had taken the laptop's blueprints and established his own company which sold these laptops! It was a crime! Sophia had even tried to sue Mark but failed. After some days, in her second attempt, his company was sued for 100 billion dollars by Sophia, as Sophia had another copy of the EcoTop blueprints were luckily with her. Mark's plan had failed. The next day, Mark disappeared without leaving a trace anywhere. He wasn't in any of his known residences and the Interpol had taken up this investigation but failed to find this fiend. The case was closed and was announced as 'inconclusive'

Sophia had reminded the Interpol about this and told them to see him as the prime suspect and told them to reopen the case, which they did do, and found out the hideout of Mark or as he was known in the underworld, BioHazard, criminal mastermind! They found out all this by hacking into the ICS or the International Criminal Syndicate's database from where they also found the whereabouts of other wanted terrorists for numerous crimes, and his ICS database, hacked by the IASFO's talented hackers. Mark had used deadly viruses to kill many people and in return he got money. He was also responsible for the Etrolola outbreak, which he admits was his greatest work ever. The next day, IASFO or the International Allied Secret Forces Organisation was launched. This was basically a union of all the secret and intelligence forces of the world. It was a part of the agreement all of the world leaders where NOMD would affect, signed. Their first task was to search – and – extract BioHazard, who was hiding in the Modern Palace, posing as Prince Duke, King of Arch, and a country independent of all continents! Oh, I forgot to mention that he was a master of disguise. Actually, all criminals are masters of disguises as that comes in their basic training! In the leaked ICS Training Package, leaked by the hackers at IASFO, it says that the list of basic things taught to these criminals include Hacking, Mixed Martial Arts, World Studies and more!

The IASFO organised a rendezvous with the mother of Prince Duke, Former Queen of Arch, Element Duke. The organisation prohibited Element to bring any mobile phones or any device which could track her. She left her home saying she was going to the Modern Church. When Duke Regal asked her why, she said she was informed that the workers wanted to meet only her to talk about the issues they were having in the modern church. They shared this secret with her and for some time, she did not believe what they were saying, but after that she admitted she saw some unusual changes in her son when they gathered for dinners, he did not eat the pizza but instead ate the Roasted Chicken Thighs with Charred Lemon Salsa Verde and Asparagus, which was accidentally cooked by the new

Royal Cook.

Actually, the royal family of Arch doesn't like Asparagus at all and so the cook could have gotten fired, but as Prince ate the dish, the cook was instead, commended on his work! This was very unusual as the Prince Duke hated asparagus and loved the pizza but still, he refused to eat it! She never asked him as she thought it was his choice and left him alone though, this still kept her bugging. Also, she noticed a clicking sound, coming from one of the rooms where she thought she saw a young lad, but there was no one there when she opened the door. She now had some belief on what they were saying and they asked her to ask her son some questions the next time they meet.

The crook was somewhere near

Hiding somewhere in fear

It was so very clear

Remember, the walls could hear!

Chapter 8

The Truth

The next phase had come, Phase 4 – Afterwave, which was basically a deadlier version of Phase 3! If the victim of this 'Afterwave' was not treated within two hours, the patient could die! Do the symptoms look a bit familiar to you? Yes, this was the .exe virus, which was suspected by Sophia and

finally recognised by Andrew Fuller, the non – evil brother of BioHazard, also known as Mark Fuller. This thing felt a bit unnatural! In fact, all of the NOMD felt unnatural! I know you need answers, what happened next? The answers were there with BioHazard and he was posing as Prince Duke. Element or Elle, as they called her, had agreed to help in the extraction of this serious offender because she knew he wasn't her son! The humanitarian group of Team X again successfully supplied the required medicines and also deployed a group of doctors who could administer the medicines the right way. Food was also, obviously supplied to the affected areas, by the IRU.

Now back to the extraction operation, which started with a beautiful morning Modern Breakfast, which would be the last Modern Breakfast the imposter would have. Elle was informed about his keen sense of smell and the knowledge he had about poisons, both of them which, were excellent. Now, he did not know about one toxin, immobilixin, unluckily as one sniff at this poisonous liquid could make you experience total immobilisation, which not only meant the complete statufication {new word – meaning immobilisation} of the muscles and bones, but multiple organ dysfunction will happen. So, somebody with the knowledge of how to administer this should be responsible of how to poison another person just enough to immobilise him, not kill him or stop him from talking!!{Otherwise, how would they catch his crimes!!?} The only known antidotes of this neurotoxin are smoke and pure water. Both of them which can help expel the toxin out of the affected human system. Elle got this information from the IASFO and had received the package from them in their recent meeting. She was told to give one drop and only one drop, in his tea and while BioHazard was as sharp as the sharpest thing in the world, he did not suspect a thing, When he drank the tea; he immediately turned into a statue {not really, he just became immobilised}. Elle then removed the mask under the culprit was hiding and voila, Mark's face popped out, She asked the agents to come inside and take him away. Duke regal was extremely flabbergasted until Queen explained everything. Later the location of Prince Duke was determined. He was found unconscious near the

tower of Parieee and was later airlifted home. They then took him to the rendezvous point, where they would meet with the other IASFO agents, which was a secret, but I'll share it with you readers. It was the Arch Bridge, where they had the Modern Secret Force Headquarters (A member of the IASFO) They interrogated him for a while, after which he confessed to his crimes. Then, Sophia asked them to bring him to her.

The fiend's destiny was set

He had become the fed's pet

What more should he get,

When his days are numbered, like the Alphabet?

Chapter 9

The Climax

Mark was taken to Switzerland on special request by Sophia. It was a not – so -long flight and with Mark being blindfolded and immobilised, he felt irritated. He was also denied of water and food, as water would neutralize the effect of the immobilixin, and we wouldn't want that now, would we? After the flight, they landed in Zurich. Mark was taken in a stretcher as he was immobilised and couldn't walk. After about 3 hours, they reached NERN. Mark was taken to Sophia, who was sitting in the LHC control room. Sophia then interrogated Mark in a bad cop tone and a heated conversation began: -

Sophia – *Now, I don't have time for this so let's finish this quickly, why did you sabotage my project.*

Mark – *Actually, you should thank me. I made your life more interesting! Without me, you wouldn't even have a 'project'.*

Sophia – *What do you mean?*

Mark – *I created the NOMD! I did all this! My friend, HackerGod, hacked into your puny SNOMDMS! I and BrainStorm made an artificial raincloud two weeks before we were actually going to initiate your so-called NOMD. We launched it into the atmosphere one week later and that's how meteorologists saw this cloud in the radar. For them, it was some kind of distant disturbance, with which they made their confused predictions. But you know what happened. After that, whatever happened was natural, the acid rain which killed thousands was only because Delhi's atmosphere was over polluted, the drought had to happen after the rain as all of the water was gone and also, the topsoil eroded. The waves of infection that, I had created. I first used the weaker version of the Ebola virus, which well killed thousands. Then, I used the .exe virus, the one you had ingested, which again killed thousands. All of these infections were in the rainclouds and these infections were designed to affect people after 2 – 3 days. The last wave is Phase 5 – Armageddon, which is basically a mega tidal wave, which will totally destroy the whole of the world! We will be away from here, in our work in progress space station!*

Sophia – *Why are you doing this?*

Mark – *This world has wronged the members of The ICS. This vendetta is the reason we wanted to destroy this planet!*

Sophia – Well, you can't if you are stuck here. Now, *tell me how to stop Armageddon and I'll let you live!*

Mark – *You can't stop Armageddon! It was designed to be unstoppable. We have already launched it! (evil laugh)*

Sophia – *Take him away! And also, mobilise him. He wont be a threat to us anymore!*

Security – *Yes, ma'am.*

(Then they mobilised him with water.)

Sophia – *Hamid!*

Hamid – *What happened?*

Sophia – *We need to deploy the Matrix Shield.*

Hamid- Why?

Sophia- Thank god we were safe about this and created these. There is a flood that will destroy the world, and it's-a-coming!

Hamid – *Locations?*

Sophia – *All of the borders of countries and shorelines of all countries.*

Hamid – *So, basically cover all of the countries by multiple Matrix Shields, right?*

Sophia – *Yes! Exactly! Now do it!*

Hamid – *Launching now!* Meanwhile, Mark was locked in an unbreakable glass chamber from which, he couldn't escape! After a while, the door was opened, but not by the security guards but by Andrew! [Turns out, he was evil as well and was planning this from a long time ago!]

He then tried to help his brother escape but just as they were nearly out of the gate and their plan almost successful, a sniper shot down both Andrew and Mark! Sophia was informed and she replied, "Well, he deserved to burn in hell. Good Job guys!"

Hamid now stood with the engineering team, who he had already briefed and they already knew what to do! Just moments before the deployment would take place, Hamid was pacing around the floor in tension and then the reverse countdown began, "10, 9, 8, 7, 6, 5, 4, 3, 2, 1, blast off!!" The deployment was successful and the domes were in place. Armageddon was going to begin in 15 minutes.

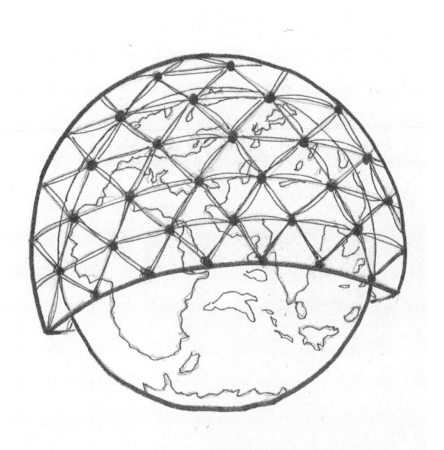

The criminal has gotten justice

The domes are in place

The happiness was bursting

And the past had become a haze

Chapter 10

Going Out With a Bang!

The large LCD – display ticking down to the beginning of Armageddon made Team X really nervous and ecstatic. Nervous because they were thinking if their plan failed, then? What if the shield wasn't as durable as it looked, then? They had no contingency plan, so now what? Ecstatic because finally, it was happening! They could become successful and famous! This created even more tension and when looking at the optimistic sides, it made them feel happier! But they felt a bit more relaxed. Hamid also gave a microphone, just in case they had to call the Army, if they were ambushed by the ICS.

Just as everyone started getting relaxed, the door opened with a loud bang. A puff of dust masked the people hiding behind it. Just as the dust cleared out, entered the ICS screaming, "Freeze!" Oh god! What were these people doing here? Then, came out a small figure, almost looking like a kid and guess what, it was a kid! Every agent of the ICS surrounded Team X and then the boss introduced himself. This is how it happened!

Master. Malevolent – *Hello, my name is Master. Mal Malevolent and I am the founder and current syndicate – king of ICS. I would love to chit chat, but you can't deploy your shields, now can you. Hackers, hack away! Guards, tie them up!*

Guards – *Yes sir!*

The thing is though, the firewalls were even more encrypted after the blackout, and even the Decrypt$nake could not destroy it. So, they desperately tried, and did not show their worries openly, but they tried. But the conversation, continued.Sophia – *What do you want from us?*

Malevolent – *I want you to let me destroy the world. I want the world to pay for the damned childhood it gave me!*

Sophia – *Your childhood is no excuse to end the world. We all have problems. But as you have decided to end the world, we have also decided something- We won't let your plan succeed, right, Hamid?*

Hamid – *Absolutely! We already knew this could happen and so we have reinforcements. Keerth, use the portable microphone I gave you. It is on!*

Keerth - *Calling TEAM XYZ, calling TEAM XYZ!*

Just then, the XYZ army tank burst in and a machine gun popped out and started shooting all of the agents of the ICS, and a battle ensued!

There was blood everywhere. Still, cold bodies everywhere… A loud, deafening sound was emitted due to this skirmish. At that exact moment, the scientists tried to go away from there but they were tied to a chair and they

couldn't escape. They were sliding their chairs and trying to exit from the back door but after that, what?! How will they run?! Don't worry guys, as Sophia already had a plan! She was also trained in survival arts and so she could survive in such a situation for at least 10 years!! What she did is she cut her rope and cut everyone's rope, which they were tied with. Then, she told everyone to walk slowly and stealthily, and they were almost out when a soldier of the ICS noticed them and shouted, "They're escaping!" The agents followed them for about a mile when the IASFO's agents shot them! Just then, their headquarters went boom! ICS was dead! Then, started the Armageddon, which was telecasted on the news everywhere. The wave hit the shield and, it just went away, deflected! It had worked at every single place! This was a victory for Team X! It was over! It was finally over!

EPILOUGE-A HAPPILY EVER AFTER AND BEYOND

A WEEK LATER

In the past week, things were very busy for Sophia and Hamid and actually, the whole of TEAM X. The adults were impressed and had already started an operation to help kids realise their dreams! The ICS was destroyed and a criminal hunt was started by the IASFO to kill the remaining criminals. The space station was repurposed into an alternate civilisation revival area, meant for the 7 billion people existing! The UC(United Congress) had released a campaign with Greentree, to create awareness of how we destroy the earth with the NOMDS created by the world, every single day. After the last press conference happened, TEAM X was sitting together, talking, in their hotel, in the LOBBY: -

Sophia – Finally, it's all over

Hamid – Yup, but now what?

Keerth – I think now, we have to go separate ways

Mohit – I don't want to lose contact with you guys!

Sophia - We won't be separated, don't worry! We'll just go to different place, but we'll always be in touch! WE ARE TEAM X AFTER ALL! Don't forget about this and each other, okay!

Everyone – OKAY!

They looked out at the moon, remembering their adventures. Just then, Keerth spotted an object that was coming towards them. In just a few seconds, it came so near, that it would seem it would crash, but then the hyper-stabilisers turned on. The vehicle stopped, and the door opened with a mysterious fog was clouding the two lifeforms, which, after the fog was lifted, was found to be human. They said in a booming voice - "Team X! We need your help! The future is in conflict and the end draws near... We need you to help us save our future!" Scared, they refused at first. But they were paragons! Always ready to save the world. Still scared, they manage to muster up the courage to hop on the weird-looking spacecraft! "Hop In!", said the two beings. It felt like the beginning of a new adventure, a new battle against an unknown threat. And the hopped in, zapping through the fabrics of time at the speed of hyperlight! What happens to them, is a tale that only time will tell!

SO, THIS WAS IT!

I HOPE THIS STORY MADE YOUR LAMPS OF CURIOSITY LIT!

THANKS, READERS!

I HOPE YOU GUYS BECOME LIGHT LEADERS!

About the Author – Arnab Sengupta

Arnab is a 15-year-old boy from India, who currently lives in the Kingdom of Bahrain. His debut book *'Iridescence – 50 Poems by a Teenage Dreamer'* notched #1 spot in the Kid's poetry section on Amazon Bestsellers. He is a pianist and one of youngest persons to have completed a semester from hallowed Berkley College of Music. He studies in Grade 10 at Bhavan's Bahrain Indian School and has won several oratory competitions, including the UNICEF-BRITMUN Best Speaker Award.

Printed in Great Britain
by Amazon

50312678R00046